A CHILDREN'S STORY BOOK

Happy
Birthday Harriet

This Series includes the following titles:

HAPPY BIRTHDAY, HARRIET!

Mr. and Mrs. Bear and their two children, Teddy and Betsy, lived in one of those houses where things go like clockwork and where there is never a speck of dust or a dirty mark to be seen. Of course, the children were not always obedient, but they seemed to make much less mess than all the other children in the same street. Take for example the Hare family who lived across the road from the Bears. There was always something going wrong, and the day I am going to tell you about, was one of the most unlucky days in the history of the Hare household.

Mummy Bear had a special job for each hour

of the day, and eleven o'clock was the time for the mid-morning cup of tea. Teddy loved this moment more than any other in the whole day, because he was allowed to have *real* tea and although it had lots of milk in it, he felt just as grown up as Daddy as he stood with his cup in his hand. When Mummy Bear had gone twice round with the teapot, she thought it was time to begin preparing the lunch, so off she went to the kitchen and started peeling apples for the children's favourite pudding — apple dumpling. She sat on a stool, humming a tune to herself and thinking about the other jobs she still had to do. Oh, yes! It was Harriet Hare's birthday and Mummy Bear wanted to make a cake to take to Harriet that afternoon. Betsy and Teddy were invited to Harriet's birthday party, so

there had to be a specially grand present to take with them.

Harriet's Mummy was working so hard, preparing for the party and also making a treat for the birthday lunch. What a lovely surprise she had for the family.... a great, big golden jelly! Mr. Hare's eyes nearly popped out of his head when he saw it, Harriet hopped up and down on her stool with delight, and Harriet's big brother, Henry, fell off his chair with excitement! Poor Henry hurt himself really rather badly and saw stars, but because it was Harriet's birthday, he didn't let a single tear fall to spoil the fun they were all having.

But oh dear me, can you guess what was happening in the kitchen while the Hare family was admiring Mummy's jelly? Harriet's birthday cake

was in the oven and Mummy had forgotten all about it. First it turned from white to yellow and then from yellow to a delicious golden brown. Then the edges began to get very, very crisp and the bottom very, very black and suddenly Mummy Hare stood still and sniffed.... "Oh, my goodness, the cake," she cried out, and ran like lightning to the kitchen. But she was far too late. When she opened the oven door, there was nothing but a cinder left and clouds of smoke were pouring out. Harriet had followed her Mummy into the kitchen, but she couldn't bear the awful smell and ran away, holding her nose, while great crocodile tears rolled down her cheeks. "Oh, my lovely cake," she sobbed, "Whatever shall we say to all my friends who are coming this afternoon. A birth-

day party without a birthday cake. Oh, oh, oh."
And Daddy tried to comfort her, but little Harriet went on crying.

Meanwhile, Mummy Bear had finished clearing up the dirty dishes from lunch and had taken her cake out of the oven. It was a prize cake. Little Betsy looked on proudly as Mummy took it out of the oven and she almost wished that they didn't have to give it away to Harriet, but could keep it all to themselves. But Betsy was very fond of Harriet and was very glad that she could take such a wonderful present to the party. Mummy then covered the cake with thick, shiney icing and put it in a box with a big, pink ribbon round it. Betsy and Teddy got into their party clothes and off they went.

When Harriet's Mummy heard what the two

little bears had brought with them, she was overjoyed. "You couldn't have chosen a better present," she said.

And she told Betsy and Teddy the story of the burnt cake. They all laughed very hard, and Teddy said: "Let's take the candles that were meant for your cake and put them on this one. Then Harriet will have a real birthday cake and won't she be surprised!"

When Harriet saw Mummy bringing it into the room, her tears disappeared and it was the happiest birthday party that you can imagine.

MR. QUACK TO THE RESCUE

Pim and Pompom were two little ginger pussy cats who were always getting into mischief. They never meant to do naughty things, but somehow or other, they could not keep out of trouble.

One day, Mrs. Puss had taken Pim with her to do the shopping. Pim loved going out with Mummy and he always got a carrot from the greengrocer when they went to buy the vegetables. Pompom, however, was in disgrace. He had been naughty, as usual, and Mummy had not allowed him to go with her. But as Pompom was sitting alone in the house, he suddenly thought of a wonderful prank to play on Mum-

my. Quickly, he ran to the cupboard and took out Daddy's fishing rod. Then he climbed onto the window-sill and waited. As Mummy came past the window, carrying her heavy shopping bag, Pompom neatly hooked a sausage out of it and hid behind the curtain. When Mummy started to unpack the parcels, she could not understand what had happened to her sausage, but then she heard a chuckle from behind the curtain and saw the fishing rod sticking out and she knew who had played a joke on her. Although she pretended to be cross, she couldn't help laughing.

"Now you two scamps," she said, "I've got to get on with the housework and I can't have you running around and getting in my way. Aunt Polly is coming to lunch so I have to make a

special treat." Now, Aunt Polly was the favourite aunt of Pim and Pompom, so they asked Mummy if they could go and fetch her with the sledge. The snow was so deep and Aunt Polly lived quite far away. Mummy was glad that they were wanting to be helpful, so of course she let them go, and she got down to cleaning the vegetables.

Next door to the Puss family lived the Quacks. Their's was a very happy-go-lucky household. Always a mess on the floor and the furniture topsy-turvy. All the same, the Quacks were a very happy family and the children were always ready to help.

It was Tuesday, and that was Mrs. Quack's baking day. She was busy making pies and cakes and scrumptious little buns. Her small

daughter, Jennifer, ladled out the dough, and Mummy rolled it into the right shape.

Daddy always helped with cooking the lunch when Mummy was busy baking. He wasn't really very fond of cooking, but he wanted to set a good example to the children, so he did his best. But the milk pudding took such a long time to cook, that Daddy thought up a good way of reading a book and stirring the pudding at the same time. He took a stool and balanced it on top of the big coal bucket. Then he leaned a ladder against the oven, climbed up the ladder and sat down. It was such a thrilling book that Daddy did not notice that the pudding was boiling over and when Jeremy Quack came into the kitchen he saw the cat having a lovely meal from the puddle of milk pudding which

was growing larger and larger every moment. How he laughed when Daddy had to mop it up! You remember that Pim and Pompom had gone off to fetch Aunt Polly in the sledge. It was a great, big, old-fashioned sledge, rather like a carriage, and Pim and Pompom had such fun taking turns, pushing each other. When at last they arrived at Aunt Polly's, she was delighted to see them. "What a grand surprise," she said. "Come along in and get warm before we set out on the return journey." So Pim and Pompom stood by the fire and drank up the cups of hot cocoa which Aunt Polly made for them. Then they packed their aunt into the sledge, with a big, soft cushion at her back and a thick rug round her legs and off they set. Pim and Pompom needed all their strength to push the

sledge, but all the same, they managed to make it go at a grand speed. In fact, Aunt Polly began to get just a little bit frightened. "Take care, children," she said. "Not too fast!" But Pim and Pompom did not listen to her warning. They bent down behind the sledge and went even faster. Now, it was almost impossible for them to see where they were going, because they could not see over the top of the sledge and they did not know that there was a fallen tree trunk lying across the road. Suddenly, Aunt Polly rang the bell furiously; ting-a-ling-a-ling, it went, but it was too late. Crash went the sledge, head-on into the tree. Over it fell into the snow, and out rolled Aunt Polly, rug and cushion and all.

Fortunately, Mr. Quack, who was by now out

skating on the nearby pond with his son Jeremy, saw the accident happen. So did Jeremy, and he fell down with the shock. But Mr. Quack quickly took off his skates and ran to the rescue. There was no real damage done and Aunt Polly was soon tucked up in the sledge again, snug and warm. Then Mr. Quack pushed the sledge to the Puss's home while Pim and Pompom ran on in advance to tell Mummy that Aunt Polly was coming.

Pompom came rushing into the kitchen where Mummy was busy making pancakes, and the first thing he said was: "We've had a crash with the sledge!" Mummy got such a fright that she tossed her pancake in the wrong direction and it landed right on Pompom's head. Then he gasped out: "But everything's alright and

Aunty will be here any moment now." Mummy was so relieved to hear that Aunt Polly was safe, that she cleaned up Pompom's face without even scolding him, and when Aunt Polly arrived, they all sat down to a delicious lunch.

When Mr. Quack got home, he was full of his story of the rescue and he was in such a good mood that he even offered to do the washing-up. "Then we'll dry the dishes," said Jennifer and Jeremy together, "and Mummy can have a rest." So Daddy washed up, without making too much mess, and Jeremy held the dishes while Jennifer dried them. And they didn't break one single thing!